To Lorraine Helen Modesitt,
whose Easter baskets were filled with love

First Aladdin Paperbacks edition January 2002
Text copyright © 1999 by Jeanne Modesitt
Illustrations copyright © 1999 by Robin Spowart

Aladdin Paperbacks
An imprint of Simon & Schuster
Children's Publishing Division
1230 Avenue of the Americas
New York, NY 10020

Designed by Anahid Hamparian
The text of this book was set in 15-point Dutch 809.
The illustrations were done in colored pencil on illustration board.
Printed in USA
2 4 6 8 10 9 7 5 3 1

The Library of Congress has cataloged the hardcover edition as follows:
Modesitt, Jeanne.
Little Bunny's Easter surprise / by Jeanne Modesitt ; illustrated by Robin Spowart. — 1st ed.
p. cm.
Summary: Little Bunny surprises her mother, father, and baby brother with Easter baskets for all of them.
ISBN 0-689-82491-2 (hc.)
[1. Rabbits—Fiction. 2. Easter—Fiction.] I. Spowart, Robin, ill. II. Title.
PZ7.M715Li 1999
[E]—dc21
98-28841
CIP
AC
ISBN 0-689-84895-1 (Aladdin pbk.)

Little Bunny's Easter Surprise

by Jeanne Modesitt   illustrated by Robin Spowart

Aladdin Paperbacks
New York London Toronto Sydney Singapore

On Easter morning Little Bunny woke up feeling especially happy. She had an Easter basket to look forward to, and this year she was going to give Mama, Papa, and Baby Brother surprises of their own.

Little Bunny hopped out of bed. She went over to Baby Brother's bed and gave the sleepy bunny a kiss.

Then she washed her face, brushed her ears, and got dressed.

She had just finished when Mama and Papa showed up at the door.

"Happy Easter!" they said, smiling.

"Happy Easter!" answered Little Bunny, with a smile of her own.

Papa's eyes twinkled. "You know, I have a feeling that somewhere downstairs there are two Easter baskets for two very special bunnies. Anybody interested in finding them?"

Little Bunny cried, "I am!"

"Me too!" said Baby Brother.

And the family went downstairs.

Little Bunny and Baby Brother found their baskets in Mama's sewing bag. Little Bunny's basket was pink, filled with little chocolate eggs, and Baby Brother's was yellow, filled with jelly beans.

Little Bunny and Baby Brother hugged their parents and said, "Thank you."

Mama smiled. "We're glad you like them."

It was Little Bunny's turn to have twinkling eyes.

"And now," she said, "you have to find *your* Easter baskets."

Mama and Papa's eyes opened wide.

"*Our* Easter baskets?" said Papa.

Little Bunny grinned. "That's right," she said. "I hid Easter baskets for everybody."

Baby Brother clapped, and the grown-ups laughed.

"What fun!" said Mama. "Let's get started."

And they did just that.

The trouble was, Little Bunny had hidden her family's Easter baskets so well, nobody could find them.

It was time for a clue.

"Ahem," said Little Bunny.

Her parents, who were searching behind the couch, looked up.

"Sometimes," said Little Bunny, "Easter baskets are hidden *outside* the house."

"Of course!" said Papa, and the family marched outside.

They looked everywhere along the ground, but still, no Easter baskets.

Another clue was definitely needed.

Little Bunny said, "Sometimes Easter baskets are hidden *above* the ground."

"Of course!" said Papa, and they began looking on top of the bushes.

Then Baby Brother said, "Pretty, pretty," and pointed at the pink blossoms on the backyard tree.

"The tree!" Mama said. Sure enough, there were three Easter baskets tucked in the tree's branches.

Little Bunny jumped up and down. "You found them! You found them!"

Mama pulled down the baskets, which were filled with eggs Little Bunny had decorated herself.

"Ooh," said Baby Brother.

"Thank you, Little Bunny," said her parents. "Your presents are beautiful."

"You're welcome," said Little Bunny. "I'm just glad you found them before *next* Easter!"

Mama and Papa laughed. Baby Brother giggled.

It was a wonderful Easter.

Later that night, as Little Bunny crawled into bed she thought, "I can hardly wait until next Easter, when I can surprise everyone again."

She lay down on her pillow and felt something hard. She lifted her pillow.

There, underneath, was one of Baby Brother's dolls, holding some of Baby Brother's jelly beans.

Little Bunny looked over at Baby Brother's bed.

And Baby Brother looked back, his eyes twinkling.

WOULD YOU LIKE TO MAKE AN EASTER BASKET FOR SOMEONE SPECIAL? HERE'S HOW:

YOU WILL NEED:

Hard-boiled eggs, watercolor paint or poster paint (make sure paints are labeled "non-toxic"), paintbrushes, white liquid glue, glitter, green construction paper, scissors, and a small container or straw basket

1. PAINT YOUR EGGS. LET THEM DRY.

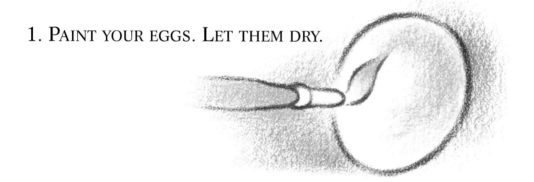

2. DRAW SOME SIMPLE DESIGNS ON YOUR PAINTED EGGS WITH LIQUID GLUE (DO ONE EGG AT A TIME). SPRINKLE THE GLUE WITH GLITTER. LET DRY.

3. CUT GREEN CONSTRUCTION PAPER INTO THIN STRIPS TO MAKE SOME GRASS. MAKE AS MUCH GRASS AS YOU NEED TO FILL UP THE BOTTOM OF YOUR BASKET.

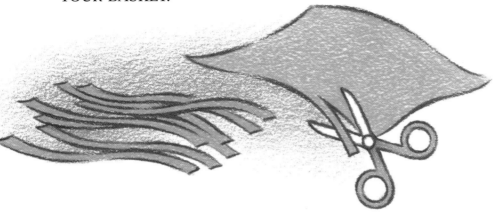

4. PUT YOUR DECORATED EGGS INTO THE BASKET.

There! Your Easter basket is now done and ready to be given to someone special. Happy Easter!